Steve Barnard has been an artist using many different media all his life. He has shown in art galleries and won awards. Steve has been featured in several e-publications as a fine artist and illustrator. Writing fiction using a very active imagination has also been combined with his ability to produce art with his own various techniques. These include sculptures, jewelry, and metalwork.

I would like to thank my wife, Marilyn, for her support and patience. She has always been one of my faithful fans. Also, my parents, Eugene and Carrol. They set the example of hard work and believing in oneself.

Steve Barnard

The Golden Harp

AUSTIN MACAULEY PUBLISHERS™
LONDON • CAMBRIDGE • NEW YORK • SHARJAH

Ordering Information
Quantity sales: Special discounts are available on quantity purchases by corporations, associations, and others. For details, contact the publisher at the address below.

Publisher's Cataloging-in-Publication data
Barnard, Steve
The Golden Harp

ISBN 9798891550803 (Paperback)
ISBN 9798891550810 (Hardback)
ISBN 9798891550827 (ePub e-book)

Library of Congress Control Number: 2023921447

www.austinmacauley.com/us

First Published 2024
Austin Macauley Publishers LLC
40 Wall Street, 33rd Floor, Suite 3302
New York, NY 10005
USA

mail-usa@austinmacauley.com
+1 (646) 5125767

I acknowledge those teachers, friends, and individuals in my life who have given me the fuel to keep the flames of creativity burning. The angels watching over me have enabled me to believe and to be thankful.

This is a story about a young man who was recruited to bring back a kidnapped granddaughter.

It's a fantasy taking place in a very make-believe setting. His challenge is so unusual and difficult.

It takes place at the bottom of a huge natural pit far away from 'civilization'. The little person, the grandfather of the young lady, has inventive skills that play a major part in her daring rescue.

Following her rescue, another adventure begins as the young man's mother is missing.

His mother has a past that connects to a diabolical scheme that she could not imagine.

– Steve Barnard

Elmer Van Pringle sat on the edge of a dusty trail, wondering why. What is it about this worn path strewn with rocks and dirty grass? How could anyone use this crude road to get anywhere? Animals surely don't walk here in search of food. There's no shade or water in sight. The cool green glade with the tall spreading trees and bright flowers was more than a couple of miles back. Elmer was getting tired and thirsty. As he arose from the knee-high rock he had been sitting on with the full intention of turning back, a small glint of sun bounced off the ground.

Suddenly excited, he bounded forward to the spot he had not taken his eyes off, certain something unusual must be lying on the ground worthy of finding. There, half covered with sand, was a gold coin! Upon closer inspection, Elmer realized he had never seen such a beautiful object. A silver angel was playing a golden harp, and on the other side was a mushroom and a castle. He must have gazed at the button-sized coin for quite a while because he noticed the sky was turning dark quickly. *Let's just see what's ahead and maybe find a clue as to where this treasure came from,* he thought. As the sun was almost hidden behind the horizon, the young man glimpsed another spark of light. There near the bottom of that tree! An old, gnarled oak with only the thickest branches remaining stood on the edge of a cliff. A dwarf-sized door with a gold knob was faintly glowing as the last beams of light reached the tree.

Elmer thought to himself it must be a mighty small person using that door. He stole up to the tree, placed his ear on it, and after hearing nothing, decided to knock softly. No sooner had his knuckles left the wood; a squeak startled him, and he quickly jumped back. The light of the sun seemed to suddenly go out.

"I know who you are, and I know where you've been." A voice said.

"Now darkness has fallen, and you want to come in."

"Who are you?" Elmerthome managed to say, wondering if he should turn around and run for his life in the dark.

"Wilford is my name, young man. In this tree I dwell, I can read the minds of good folk like you but not evil ones, and it's probably just as well."

The small stranger looked deep into the much taller youth's eyes as if to read his very soul.

"Don't be afraid, my friend," the little man said.

"Come in; I'm sure you can squeeze through my door. I'll even offer my hand to lend." Elmer managed to barely fit into the doorway. Once inside, he cautiously stood up to a sort of half crouch. After going down four dinky steps, he could stand upright in a kind of cave. A few candles showed it had a dirt floor. It was very neat and clean, and there was a large table with little else for furniture.

"Help yourself to some fresh-baked mushroom cookies," Wilford said as he held out a small shiny plate. The sweet smell of pastry reached his nose, the warm cookies made him remember his mother, and suddenly he felt homesick.

"I know," Wilford said as Elmer found a small stool to sit on gently so as not to break it.

"Your mother, with whom you live alone, will be worried when you don't come home. I've read your mind, and I know you have three days before she will be expecting you. That should be enough time to plan and finish our rescue."

"Rescue?" Elmer asked; the possibility of new excitement made him wiggle on his chair.

"What kind of rescue, where, how, who!"

"Now, now, now," Wilford said in a calming voice. "First thing in the morning, we shall get down to the details. You need to sleep because I'm afraid there is not going to be much time for rest until the job is done."

When daylight filtered into Elmer's eyes, he could make out the form of Wilford preparing breakfast; the sweet smell of frying mushrooms hit his nose. What a strange little man he had found. Elmer and felt the warmth of a friendly place.

The adventure! The memory of last night filled his mind, and Elmer jumped up. "Yes, I know you want to get started, but first come and have something to eat."

Wilford really could read his mind, and it was rather scary.

"Don't worry, young man; I would never know your thoughts if you didn't want me to." Elmer was relieved to hear this news and felt a nice trusting feeling. He just knew they were going to be great friends. His host brought two plates piled high with pancakes and mushrooms as well as honey and fruit juice.

"Eat hardy, big guy, for today you're going to learn how to fly."

"And tomorrow, you'll know the reason why."

"What did you say?" Not knowing where those words came from, Elmer asked.

"Oh yes, Elmer, I can also send you my thoughts. I can only do that with a few good people."

"WOW! But for now, can we just talk normally? I'm getting a little dizzy with all this new stuff." "Sure, Elmer, finish your breakfast, and then I'll show you something that will really take your breath away," he said, or Elmer thought he said.

As he finished his breakfast, Elmer realized he was next to a window. (In a cave?) He thought that was odd. Standing up, he could see a walkway leading to a platform suspended in the air.

"Okay, let's go outside and see what we've got," Wilford said with a serious voice.

"Look here!" His new friend said as Elmer walked to the edge of the outside balcony and looked down. As far as he could see, there were other balconies, decks, and porches. Farther down, a few lanterns disappeared into a deep, dark hole in the earth. The 'hole' was about five hundred feet across and half a mile deep.

"What's down there?" Elmer asked, catching his breath and then moving back, remembering his fear of heights.

"It's a city of sorts," Wilford said. "Only this one goes sideways down the walls of the cliff instead of flat like most towns on the surface of the earth."

Wilford paused and waited for Elmer to form his next question and then answered without waiting for the words.

"Yes, someone does live at the bottom of this shaft, an evil king who kidnapped my granddaughter!" Wilford's face took on a red sour expression, one Elmer thought the elf could never make.

"Now close your eyes, and I will reveal to you the whole story in your mind."

When the sun shone directly overhead and cast its beam down the shaft, all the cliff dwellers watched as the huge diamond, which was mounted on the top of a golden harp, lit up the pit from far below in a sudden flash of brilliant, blinding rainbows.

About once a month, Bailey played the golden harp. Its familiar refrain of crystal notes started out small and crisp. As they rose out of the center upward to the rim of the crater, they increased in volume and fullness like a giant horn. The sound traveled ever skyward and ricocheted up to the thousands of captive listeners, the cliff people. To them, it was pure musical ecstasy. They lived only for the time when the "Silver Princess," As they called her, would play for them. Each one of them was destined to dig in the dark with only a small candle attached to their hat to see with. The treasure they sought was gold. Nuggets of it would sparkle in the weak light, just waiting to be collected. Then, the gold was saved until each person had so much they could barely carry it.

Then, it was hauled to a large cavern and melted together. The King's men who oversaw the operation made sure the gold was cast and polished into beautiful gleaming coins. Wilford related to Elmer how the king had not only discovered gold but also uncovered a huge diamond the size of a watermelon. But instead of selling it for enough money to buy a whole county, he devised a plan to get even richer. It was simple: kidnap children from far away so in the search for them would also be far away. Then, put them in the natural caves by way of a secret tunnel. That was the easy part. King Otar knew that to reap as much gold as possible, he would need to motivate the young miners; otherwise, they would be lazy, and there wouldn't be enough of his frightening soldiers to keep them all working. Why could he become richer than even the two sisters who lived on an island he had heard about? No one knew where the island was, but everyone from the age of understanding said they practically ran the world. Music! That was the key! If there is one thing that does rule the world in many ways, it is the beat of life set to the rhythm of the stars and the singing of the oceans with the melody of mountains and forests, all composed by the sun, wind, and rain.

Otar had heard of a young girl who played the harp so wonderfully that all musicians, past and present if put together, could not compare. He knew such a person would be his answer, and the plan was working soon after he had stolen Bailey from her home. When Bailey played, and the last notes of the beautiful golden harp faded away into thin air, the miners gave up their treasures, hoping to hear more. There was a cascade of gold raining down to the bottom of the pit. Highly polished gold coins with skillfully crafted engravings of the harp and the Princess. These coins were the result of many hours of hard and tedious labor; they were all the children had to offer for the reward of heavenly music. Otherwise, the only sound heard for weeks at a time was the muffled scratching of their digging. They learned to mimic the notes from the harp in a humming sound.

Wilford spoke, "Bailey is her name, and no creature so beautiful has ever lived. She is as gentle as soft rain on a mountain meadow. She dances like spring flowers waving in the breeze."

"You must help me rescue her, Elmerthome." Elmer opened his eyes and felt a sadness overcome him. He knew he just had to rescue Bailey and set the children free, but how could he? Wilford read his mind and pointed to his funny-looking airplane. The plane was too small for the young man to even sit in, much less hold his weight during flight.

"Don't worry, Elmer, Wilford said. I figure we can cut a hole in the bottom so you can sit down and hang your feet through and maybe add another wing." Elmer had his doubts. "What about the tiny engine?" he asked, feeling there was something his short friend had forgotten. He could not imagine this small flying machine carrying him safely any place and back. Wilford replied to those thoughts.

"Back? No, you won't be able to fly up with the extra weight of Bailey."

"Well, how am I to get all the way back here?" Elmer asked.

"I'm afraid the only way out will be by tunnel," Wilford replied.

"What tunnel?" Elmer asked, knowing this might be more of an adventure than he bargained for.

"Well..." Wilford said, drawing the word out to give himself time to think of a good answer.

That night. Elmer was gliding down past the city. There were no streets in this town, and instead of lampposts, there were only dim yellow glows from candles. These were made from twisted moss and mushroom stems. Wilford had told him that without the lowly mushroom, the poor kids would not have food or light. Elmer saw their eyes behind the flickering flames as he descended past the narrow ledges. These were their homes. As Elmer flew closer to the bottom, he could see the sparkle of gold. A small mountain of coins like the one he had found only yesterday was heaped around the solid gold harp, with the diamond giving off a warm glow like a crystal lantern. All this was part of the castle built on a rock archway shooting up hundreds of feet from the cavern floor. He thought he saw Bailey. A small girl was lying on a pile of straw, but he wasn't sure, so he got closer. The closer he flew, the nearer because no one could hear the silent plane or see him in the dim light. So close a sleeping dragon smelled Elmer Van Pringle.

"SNAP!" The Dragons' teeth barely missed Elmer's exposed legs.

"WHOA! Wilford never said anything about a mean old dragon!" he yelled out loud.

Just then, the King's army was alerted by the ruckus and came out from all around the castle. Elmer had no choice but to land and be captured. As he sat in the dungeon waiting for the King's decision on what to do with him, the sound of the harp reached his ears. The music was so clear and beautiful. Elmer started to cry just at the sound of it. Then, he was filled with such joy and excitement he felt his chest would burst. And then silence.

Suddenly, the sound was deafening, a sound like metal rain. With such a clamor, Elmer's ears hurt as pure gold coins landed on top of other gold coins. The ringing, stinging, zinging noise tapered off into a still quiet. The jail door opened. A deep voice in a grunting manner said, "Ugh, ugh!" Elmer cautiously took a step out of the dark cell and was immediately pushed along a wet hallway. After a long walk, the man who had been behind him grabbed him by the shoulder and said, "Ugh."

The huge stinky man knocked on a door then opened it and threw Elmer into a room. A small animal came out and sniffed at Elmer's legs.

"Stand up you!" Said a raspy voice.

It was a large bedroom with a dumpy, grumpy man sitting up in bed. Omer felt as if he was going to faint. The small animal that was checking him out was a bird that flew up and landed on his head.

"HA, HA, HA!" The king laughed so hard he nearly fell out of his bed.

"All right, young man, Eyeball likes you, so you must be okay."

Elmer could tell this man was evil and didn't trust him at all.

"How about we take a stroll out to the patio and introduce you to the lovely lady responsible for this wonderful mountain of gold." The guard stayed just out of earshot but close enough that he could grab Elmer if he tried to run. Grunt, that would be a good name for this bad guy, he thought, since that's all he ever said. After a climb up some dark stairs, a clanking chain raised a large wooden door. Torchlight steamed into Elmer's eyes, hurting them. Once his sight adjusted to the scene, and he was able to see where he stood, Elmer's breath was sucked away by the view. They were on top of a huge natural pinnacle that formed a huge tower far above a blue pond surrounding it.

"I've brought you some company, my dear." Said the king, whose eyes could not really stand the light. They were accustomed to the faint glow of candles and darkness inside the castle. He shielded his eyes and stood back from the opening; then, without another word, the heavy door slammed shut with a deafening crash. Elmer was amazed at how long it took for the echoes of the noise to fade. In fact, it was a minute before he was able to speak.

"Hello," Elmer said a little too loudly, not realizing how easily it was amplified to a shout.

"Hello," Bailey whispered.

A growl came from the far side of the terrace. It started like a meow of a kitten and grew until it was louder than a lion. They were so loud they had to cover their ears to keep them from popping!

"We must be quiet or Quasar, we'll be having you for dinner. By the way, my name is Bailey." With a slight curtsy of her ragged dress, Elmer knew he had fallen in love. The fresh as snow in the morning with the warmth of a cozy fire kind of love that only comes once in a lifetime.

Meanwhile, King Otar shuffled back to his bed, where he spent most of every day and night. He ordered his favorite snack, scrambled eggs, and popcorn. Eyeball, his pet bird, sat on the bedpost and waited for a stray morsel of food.

"Well, Eyeball, what do you think of our new friend? I believe he'll make a good drummer boy. We should be able to collect much more gold with the added sound of a booming drum." The king, with a full tummy, nodded off and dreamed of mountains of gold topped with ice cream and spaghetti.

That night, as Elmer and Bailey sat on the edge of the stone floor with their legs dangling into space, not much was said. The feeling of empty quiet was overwhelming. Bailey had long since given up any hope of escape. Elmer himself felt despair creeping into his own thoughts. Was he to end up here as a prisoner for the rest of his life as Bailey had resigned herself to? He nudged her and whispered, "Hey." She smiled but didn't reply. The poor girl had nearly forgotten how to speak to another person. She really had nothing to talk about. Her world was limited to days of sitting on a rock waiting for King Otar to ring a bell signaling her to play the harp. Oh, what a harp! Elmer looked over at the gold harp and was amazed at the size of it. It was as large as a house is tall. The moonlight showed through the diamond and made a rainbow of sparkling light dance across the floor. It was inviting, even beckoning Elmer to walk closer. The silver ribbon-like strings stretched skyward, drawing him closer. In a soft tiptoe, Elmer moved nearer, then slid easily onto the tall stool and paused briefly before reaching out and barely touching a string. A warm tone sounded as if the harp were alive, aware of Elmer and begging him to continue.

The soft hand of Bailey touched his shoulder. He turned and could see her face inches from his.

"Let me play you a song." She said as she glided in next to him and began to play. It seemed like a lullaby from long ago, something Elmer couldn't quite remember. A melody so sweet it had the feel of Mother Earth herself. The notes were so clear he felt he could cup his hand and catch each one before they could spread out like water ripples in space. The sound magnified as each note swelled and then broke apart into countless pieces and floated upward to the poor miners.

King Otar awoke from his deep sleep as he heard the notes from the harp.

"What the devil is going on? I didn't tell her to play!" He shouted and ran down the hall. With one pull of his short arms and pudgy body, he jerked the chain that opened the heavy door and rushed out onto the moonlit deck. Even the dim light so far below the surface hurt his eyes. Elmer saw the king was blinded and used the few seconds to race over to the open doorway. He heard the echo of Grunt pounding towards them in the dark hall, searching for his master. Quasar, the dragon, was starting to stir! Elmer sprang back and grabbed the dazed Bailey and had to drag and push her to the door.

Fowl dragon-breath and then fire dragon-breath reached Elmer's neck. Grunt saw them, turned, and lunged with a wild grab as they pushed past him. He turned around, looking for the king, and caught dragon fire in the face as the large door crashed shut.

The two ran frantically down many dark passages, looking for a way to escape. Finally, they got outside and found a grass courtyard beside a clear blue pond. Breathless, they collapsed and slowly realized their captor was now the captured. It would be the next day before the guards discovered their king was missing and started hunting for the two of them.

"Let's just sleep for a while, Elmer," Bailey said.

And so, they slept on the soft grass beside the yellow sand and blue water.

Peck, peck, peck. Elmer woke up and found he was eyeball to eyeball with Eyeball! "Well, hello there, little buddy, you wouldn't happen to have some food. I'm starving!" "Me too!"

Said Bailey, who had stood up and stretched.

"Shush, I think I hear someone coming!" She said suddenly.

King Otar was on their trail with large animals. They had big noses and sharp claws, mole-like creatures that ate stray miners.

"Let's go into one of these caves and get away from them," Elmer said.

"Yeah, I guess we don't have a choice," Bailey said, not really wanting to go into the unknown darkness. There was no time to choose from the many caves. They ran straight to the nearest one. They heard footsteps and voices that seemed to be getting closer. They stumbled and fell many times, too tired to go on but too scared to stop. After what seemed like an hour, they could go no further. They fell to the ground, exhausted and breathing heavily, fearing they had been swallowed up by the earth and certain death. In the excitement, they had lost Eyeball. Sleep again came. The darkness inside of more darkness, a slumber so thick and near-fatal, until a yellow light barely edged its way under Bailey's soft eyelids. She grabbed Elmer by the arm, yelled, jumped up to her feet, and pulled him up before he knew what was happening. They rushed towards the glowing light, and as they approached it, they both bumped into a hard object. Elmer knew it was a door, and the light was coming from underneath it. Was it locked? Had they perhaps blundered back to the wicked King's chambers?

Elmer gave it a slight push, and it cracked open. They both waited, staying perfectly still, not wanting to take a chance on being captured again. A snoring sound came from the room. Elmer whispered, "I'm going in." Inside the room was a person sitting in a small chair. Bailey followed quietly. As their eyes adjusted to the mushroom lamp, the person woke up and spoke.

"Ooze there?"

"Who are you?" Elmer demanded.

"Jez me," said a suddenly scared voice. "I wuz only restin' honest."

Bailey could tell it was the voice of a girl, very frightened, and so she said softly, "Don't be afraid we won't hurt you."

"No, we are trying to find a way out," Elmer reassured her.

"Oh, thank even I thought you were the King's guard." The girl sighed with relief.

"What's your name?" Elmer asked.

"Gee, I dun't think I remember."

"What? Don't remember your own name!" Elmer replied.

"Well, you might furget it too if you had been down there forever with no one to talk to or call your name!" She snapped and then burst into tears.

"I'm sorry," Elmer said and took a step closer and touched her shoulder.

"It's Sue or Blue or something."

Bailey said, "It must be Sue; Blue is a silly name."

"NO IT IS BLUE 1 REMEMBER NOW!"

"Are you sure?" Elmer said, not believing her.

"Of course, you think I don't know my own name?"

They sat in silence for a moment. Blue was the first to speak.

"I've gotta go back and find some more gold so I can 'ear the Princess play." It took Bailey a second before she realized that she was The Princess.

Bailey spoke, "Blue, I am the Princess."

The lonely little girl did not know what to say; she felt almost cheated. Deep inside, she sensed all that she had been living for was gone. No more heart-warming music, nothing to live for. She wiped her tears and sat down for a minute.

"Well, there's only one thing we can do to find our way to the top," Blue said. "Find the secret tunnel; that's how we got here, but the moles might find us first."

Elmer thought it best to strike out by himself to look for the only passage to the surface and leave the girls to recruit other miners. A larger number would have a much better chance of finding a way before King Otar and his men caught up with them. He wandered a long time before coming upon a steep trail. It twisted and turned upwards until it stopped suddenly at a large gate with a chain and lock. He grabbed the gate and shook it. He knew he had found the only tunnel to freedom. But without the key, there simply was no way past the obstacle.

"I've got to go back to the castle," he explained to Bailey when he saw her at the meeting spot they had arranged. "I'll get the key and be back for you."

"No, Elmer, you will be captured!" Bailey said, knowing it was no use trying to talk him out of it.

It really was the only thing to do.

"Let us come too!" said a bunch of kids excited and a chance to help but still fearful of the man who treated them so terribly.

"No, thank you. I'll be better able to sneak into the King's room by myself." Elmer reasoned.

Wilford sat by his window, looking out and down into the abyss. He knew Elmer would be able to rescue his beloved granddaughter even though it was too far for him to make mind contact; he felt Bailey was now safe, and it was just a matter of time before she returned. It had been two years since Bailey had disappeared. Wilford immediately started searching and spent a couple of months before he got a clue as to where she was. Some passing hunters had heard music coming from what they described as a canyon. He had built his small airplane in hopes of flying down to the bottom of the place to investigate. Little did he realize the real danger until he saw the dragon and armed guards. And there, helpless and frail, was Bailey. Wilford knew he had better not try another flight because they would be ready to capture him, and then all hope really would be lost. And now the answer to his prayers, a young lad just perfect for the job, came along. *All Elmer needs to do*, he thought, *is find the right tunnel, and I can send them mental directions for the others to follow.* Wilford drifted off to a blissful sleep and dreamed of flying low over fields of fragrant clover.

That night, Elmer did go back and was lucky the guards weren't expecting him. He sneaked his way up to the very doorway of King Otar's bedroom and crept in. He dropped to his stomach and crawled over to the dresser, stood up, and searched each drawer. It must have taken half an hour, being careful not to make a single sound.

Darn, no luck. Elmer decided to take a big chance and make his way to the bedside table. What if the king had the key around his neck?

Elmer made up his mind if he had to, he would snatch the key and race for freedom. He slithered across the large room and froze when he nearly bumped into the King's fancy boots. You see, Elmer had noticed there were bells on them, and the sound would surely have awakened Otar. But wait! There on one boot was a gold key hanging by a tassel. *That must be the one*, he thought.

Elmer quickly cut the cord and could barely keep from jumping up and dashing back to the tunnels. He shivered with terror when his groping fingers felt the cold, slimy skin of the king's sleeping alligator at the foot of the bed. One false move, and he would be an Elmer burger.

Finally, he backtracked and found his friends anxiously awaiting his return. They were just as happy he was safe as they were to know Elmer had the key to their freedom. Once they got past the gate, it wasn't much further until the tunnel opened into a sloping hill with small trees just below the top edge of the pit. Elmer gave Bailey a hand up to the surface where they could at last stand and see the flat ground stretching to the yonder mountains. They looked at each other and burst out laughing; the dim light in the tunnels didn't show the dirt and grime that had stuck to their faces. It was quite funny to see the whites of their eyes peering out. In fact, all the former captives were laughing and cheering. Elmer and Bailey were very tired after the long climb and goodbyes. The sun was almost down, just as it was when he had first found the gold coin. He remembered that in his pocket now was a leather bag with a wealth of gold he was going to take home to his mother. Bailey had a gold necklace fashioned from the coins the grateful miners made for her.

It was dark when they used the last bit of candles to find Wilford's tree. Of course, the small man was waiting for them outside, and with tears of joy, he hugged Bailey and then Elmer. After a brief cry and more hugs, they went inside to wash up and eat freshly baked Raisin cookies. In the morning, before saying their goodbyes and promises to see each other again soon, Wilford said to Elmer.

"I have just the thing to get you home in a blink." He smiled at Elmer and gave him a wink. On the back porch was a sleek new red airplane.

"WOW!" said Elmer.

"You had better get in and fly, or we'll never say goodbye." Bailey rhymed for a change. She held his hands and gave him a big kiss. Elmer turned red but quickly kissed her again. He climbed into the plane and found it fit perfectly. He fired up the engine and, with a wave, was off in the direction of home. Then, as he didn't think anything could be more perfect, Eyeball flew up and landed beside him.

Meanwhile, the King's kingdom was fast dissolving. He had to devise a way to gather the gold and take it to his other castle. He summoned all his men and ordered them to start packing it to the top. It took them many days of constant work. When it was finished, Otar dragged his out-of-shape, lazy self out of the gold mine. He was shocked to find the massive treasure had been hauled off.

"Stolen! How dare they!" He shouted.

The King, with no loyal subjects, was alone. Even his pet bird, Eyeball, had betrayed him.

As he walked around wondering what to do, he came across the tree that had once been Wilford's home. He saw the door and thought perhaps there would be food inside. A King's appetite is never filled, and the long walk up through the mine tunnels only made it worse. He opened the door, got on his knees, and proceeded to crawl in. But halfway in, his large belly and overstuffed money-belt got him quite stuck. You might say King Otar got his just dessert. He died there, unable to free himself.

Wilford and Bailey left shortly after Elmer flew off. They loaded down the donkey Ben with their meager belongings and headed for the lake country where their real home was. Bailey got so excited when she saw her grandmother and her childhood friends. She did not miss that big, beautiful harp at all or the mean old king who took her away. She loved the nice wooden harp her grandfather made for her, and it sounded just fine!

Wilford went back to his small, neat workshop where he loved to tinker away the days. His favorite project was making flying machines like the one he quickly made for young Elmer while he was busy saving Bailey. He picked out a hammer among the row of them hanging above his head. He tapped gently on the piece he was working on and thought of Elmer and wondered if he was all right. Putting the hammer back, for he never left a tool out of place, Wilford made a sudden decision to visit his pal.

"Jet-Pac, Rocket-Belt, Sky-Car, one of those will get me there no matter how far," Wilford said to Cosmo, the cat lying in the sun on his back, dozing as usual.

"Tomorrow, we leave for Black Mountain."

As Elmer banked the flying machine towards Black Mountain, he hoped to be home before nightfall. He could almost see his mother's eyes now as he imagined walking through the door and giving her a big hug. It had been over a month since he had left to go fishing, and he knew she would be very, very worried. The landing wheels had barely touched the ground before Elmer was running up to the front door and racing into the warm, familiar kitchen, expecting to throw his arms around his mom and quickly explain what made him so late. He thought it might take a whole week to tell her all that had happened.

"Mom, I'm home," Elmer yelled as he burst into the house.

Silence

"MOM!"

Elmer sensed something was different or wrong. He knew his mother would be home as it was almost dark, but where was she?

He searched for a note and then peered out the window, thinking perhaps she was in the garden. Then he noticed a very odd thing. The purple shawl Elmer had given his mother, the one she never left home without, was lying on the floor.

Elmer was so distraught he couldn't sleep. All night in the cold, lonely house, he could only pace the floor, not bothering to go to bed. He finally sat down and wondered where his mother could be. *I've got to fly over to Aunt Marilyn's and see if she knows anything*, he thought. A feeling of panic and then fear followed by loneliness came over him. Just as he was leaving, he noticed something was missing: his mother's family photo album. The one with the silver cover was placed with care on the fireplace mantle. "WOW, something really is wrong!" He blurted it out loud. "Come on, Eyeball, we've got to go!" The bird was outside, sitting on the fence, making friends with the neighborhood birds.

Tommy has been gifted since he was a young boy. He could build things from his mind's eye that were far advanced, even for adults. He thought of all the flying machines he had made so far; he had one in mind that was a grand design that he wanted to build. It was an airship that was large enough that one could live on it. Tommy Wilford was about to manufacture something that had never been imagined by anyone else. Everyone always called him Wilford instead of his first name, Tommy. He realized he would need help to build such a large flying ship. He knew of a family called the Bubblebots. They lived on an island they had built on a lake several generations ago as an escape from the normal world. It was a large manufacturing complex. Each of them had special skills that were only dreamed about by other craftsmen. They worked quickly, following Wilford's plans. It helped tremendously that he could communicate to them by thought as they worked without needing drawings on paper. When it was finished, they all stood back and admired such a beautiful machine. It had a living cabin suspended from an air balloon pointed on both ends. Underneath the capsule was a jet engine powered by the most cutting-edge fuel technology.

Wilford did not know how valuable it was to be on his trip to visit Elmer.

Wilford and Bailey were excited about the idea of visiting Elmer as a surprise. They didn't know that he had left in a hurry to find his mother, Edna. And so, when they arrived, there was no sign of Elmer or his plane. They entered the house; the front door was open, but the house was empty. "It looks like something has disturbed this peaceful little cottage," Wilford said. Bailey was very worried and started to cry. "How can we ever find where he is and his mother?"

They got back on the airship, and with Wilford's mental powers, he discerned which direction Elmer had flown. Once Wilford's radar spotted what must be Elmer's airplane, he raced full speed ahead to catch up. Elmer noticed a strange-looking flying object behind him. Wilford flashed his lights, and Elmer slowed down so that whoever it was could catch up. After making contact, they landed. It was a happy reunion with hugs and the big grins on their faces.

"Come aboard, my friend, and see what I and the Bubblebots have made." They were amazed at the complex design and exquisite craftsmanship of every detail inside and out of the flying wonder. It was Wilford's finest creation. It was fully equipped to fly around the world. "How is it that you know how to build such a marvelous machine?" Elmer asked.

No one knew that Wilford had once been a janitor at a large rocket company. And even though he had no formal education, he had a sponge-type brain. Every tossed-out scrap of paper or formula left on a blackboard, every overheard technical conversation, was all filtered through his clever mind. Eventually, he could no longer live in the city, and besides Bailey's parents disappeared, she needed grandparents. And so, it was from the age of four that Bailey soon adapted to her new home and schoolmates, and Wilford and Helga, his wife, settled into the role of parents.

The next day, it was decided Wilford's flying machine would take the lead. Elmer would be behind alone as Bailey wanted to be with her grandpa. All went well until they started having trouble.

"Grab the wheel!" Wilford shouted. Bailey had never heard such fear in her grandfather's voice. The fright transferred to her very being and found its way to her fingers. They trembled and turned white as she struggled to hold on to the spinning control wheel. An emergency landing was necessary and quick! After a near-crash landing, they felt lucky to be alive. Wilford found the problem. Some animals had worked their way into the cable system; they made a nest that eventually clogged up the steering controls.

Oskar Cottonwood lived alone and was fixing lunch when he heard a whining sound above the treetops. He strained his ears and looked up, wondering what on earth could that be. Oskar hid under a tree branch and peered out in the direction of the commotion. And then he saw a banana-shaped balloon with an engine. He heard panicked voices getting closer. He cautiously crept up to get a closer view after it landed. Such an extravagant airplane or blimp or whatever it was, Oskar could never have imagined.

Wilford sensed someone was watching them. He called out, "Who's there?" It was more of a command than a question. It had been a long time since Oskar had heard a voice other than his own. He had long ago decided to leave civilization and live out his days in peace and away from other people. Suddenly, he felt a rush of anxiety, thinking he should just go back to his shelter and pretend this never happened. Bailey decided to investigate whoever must be watching them. Before her companions could stop her, she was out of sight and cautiously stepping towards the smell of cooking. Oskar had gone back to his tiny kitchen. It had just enough space to cook on a makeshift fire pit. All his utensils and dishes were fashioned from bits and pieces of rocks and wood fragments. He had decided to just ignore the intruders, although he was very curious as to what they were up to. Bailey crept up to the opening of his meager abode.

"Hello." She spoke.

"AAHHH!" Oskar screamed. He was so shocked to hear a female voice and let out a yell so loud that Wilford and Elmer came running.

"Whatcha wants?" Oskar whined, scared and shaking. Just then, her two friends barged in and grabbed Bailey to protect her from this stranger. Oskar stood there boldly but defensively. His orange-red hair was neatly pulled back into a ponytail. His face was haggard, full of lines, with a ragged gray beard.

"I say we're not here to harm you," Wilford said.

"Go away!" Oskar said in a pleading voice. After a few minutes, they all warmed up to each other, knowing they could be friends. He explained why they were there and apologized for interrupting Oskar's day. Oskar was fascinated with the new technology aboard the airship. The longer he stayed to visit, the more he realized that he really did need people to talk to. To lessen the tension among them, Oskar pulled out his harmonica and began to play an old blues tune. Bailey, with her musical talent and soft lilting voice, began to hum and then sing. Wilford kept the banjo handy and joined in with Elmer, keeping time with a spoon on a tin can.

Edna was confused as to why some strange people had abducted her for no apparent reason. At first, she thought it must be a joke, but then reality set in, and she panicked, thinking she might never see Elmer again. Her son was missing, and now she would be missing when he got home. As she was riding in the back of a plane, it was very comfortable. The only sound was the plane engine, which was loud. If only she had something to do, such as knitting or reading. For some reason, they had brought with her the silver book of her family history.

Carrol and Rosie walked out onto the bridge connecting their castles on Oracle Island. They anxiously awaited the arrival of their guest. Edna was sleeping when the aircraft landed. Her cabin door opened, and someone said, "We're here."

Edna stepped out wearing the same dress with no shoes, just as she had been when she was taken. Both ladies approached Edna with their hands extended in a welcome gesture. Edna said nothing as it was explained to her why she was taken from her home several days ago. However, Carrol and Rosie refrained from the whole story.

Edna knew there was more that wasn't being told to her. Her thoughts of her son Elmer missing for so long brought her to tears. She sobbed, tightening her fists, and spoke.

"HOW DARE YOU DO THIS TO ME? I'm just a poor woman trying to survive with little means and simple wants!" Carol moved to take Edna's hand and reassured her she was in no danger.

After a week, Edna noticed Carol and Rosie walking out of their doors, facing the suspended bridge connecting them to each crystal sphere. Just before sunrise, they would meet at the center, each standing on a crystal step. Holding each other's hands, they would look straight down into the silver surface of the Oracle. Edna did not know that when the sun's first rays struck the ball, a clear vision of the whole world events for the coming week would be revealed. Every major influence had to do with politics, wars, and economics, as well as scientific and medical discoveries, global warming, population shifts, pollution, and election results. Only the most vital information that was affecting the earth was focused on for a few minutes. All this information was useless unless it could be manipulated. Carol and Rosie were masterminds at controlling a few of the events, but they wanted more!

Oracle Island was two towers jutting up from the ocean floor. At some point in time, a sunspot magnetic storm sent a comet consisting of uranium, chromium, carbide, aluminum, magnesium, and diamond particles into the Earth's atmosphere. It had been pulled off course by the sun's gravity; it was moving at nearly light speed. As it rounded the sun's perimeter, the path changed direction towards earth. It had a 50-mile white hot tail. It entered the ocean at the precise point of the dead center of the earth. The depleted uranium formed a needle-like point that was rooted in the molten core of the earth. It combined with the earth's minerals and oxygen and formed two huge lava towers.

Both spires produced bubbles at the top. They were clear as glass, emerging from the water. The hollow crystal balls cooled as they sat on top of the two spires. The purity and the curved surfaces made them invisible to modern-day radar.

Days went by until Edna could not stand the mystery. "Okay, you two, I am fed up and demand that you tell me how long I am going to be here and why," Edna asked, breaking out in tears, fearing to hear bad news. She stormed off to her room and stayed there until she was so hungry she ventured out. She found them arguing with each other rather violently. The sisters looked at Edna. She was ready to explode; her face was purple. Edna could see this could be dangerous and wanted no part in it.

Carol and Rosie realized it was time to explain the details. Rosie cleared her throat. "We will take you back after we explain who you really are. Do you remember your parents or your childhood?" Edna's face went blank. She had no memory until she was in her early twenties.

"Why should you care? My past belongs to me!" Rosie took over the conversation.

"Well, once we explain your background and your heritage, you may not want to return to your simple, dreary life. In your family history book, have you noticed a large gap in time?"

"Why yes, it does show only Father's history for the last 500 years."

Rosie said, "There's a reason your mother's side was left out, and it goes back beyond 500 years."

Edna was shocked! "How could you know anything about my genealogy?" She asked.

Rosie spoke with a serious tone.

"Your line of grandmothers goes back to a very special lady. SHADOW was the name given to the newborn girl so long ago."

Her powers were carried on with every first-born girl; however, at one point in time, twin girls were born. Edna began to realize the seriousness of her trip to this strange place. She sat tense, her throat closed, and she began to choke; Edna fainted. When woke up, the story continued.

Shadow happened to be born under what is known as A BAD SIGN. The exact moment she was born was also the only time in which the sun was blacked out. A meteor so large and at the perfect distance from the Earth it cast a black shadow over the entire planet. The instant flash of blinding, glaring fierceness of its power was too much for an eye to adjust to. It was several days later before people and animals began to get their sight back.

Shadow was such an unusual baby from the very beginning. She seemed to know exactly what her mother was doing. She didn't cry at all. Her mother was always there at her side to take care of her needs. Even when her mother was doing chores, she would stop and go pick up Shadow and feed or change her because it was as if the baby could send her thoughts.

Shadow could speak as well as an adult before her fourth birthday. She figured out how sounds were made with each spoken word and memorized the basic construction of speech.

She was so unusual many people thought she was an evil spirit. As she began to foresee the future of individuals around her, the special gift spread like wildfire. Shadow was the very first fortune teller. Her family kept her away from everyone, and so she lived cut off from her village.

When she was old enough to leave home, she began to travel the world. Shadow helped those she met by seeing a person's future and enabling them to alter their choices. Often, it was a blessing for them. If they decided to go ahead and change their path, it could not be undone. Shadow moved on, having bestowed the gift of seeing the future. With her foresight, she knew which person she met needed the fortune the most.

She did not look like an ordinary woman. She had long, silken black hair and wore bones and beads in it. Her skin glowed like the sunset; her green eyes and long lashes would mesmerize you into a hypnotic state of peace. Sometimes, her eyes would change to orange. These were times when Shadow went into another world. The information her brain was receiving at these times would overwhelm her nervous system. When she came out of this trance, she was the most powerful.

Edna was exhausted after Carol and Rosie had told the history as told to them so many generations ago.

"So, what does this have to do with me?" Edna said.

Rosie looked at Carol and walked close to Edna. Carol stayed back with her arms folded.

The sisters had rehearsed Edna's question many times. They knew Edna would have trouble believing such a bizarre connection to herself. However, it was vitally important that Edna would accept this story as fact. Rosie began to speak.

"Shadow lived to be well beyond 150 years old. All the children that followed were females."

"Many generations of baby girls lived and died, each having only one girl themselves."

Edna felt anxiety flooding her body; she was disassociated with the story at first. But to believe there were no boys born for so many years, Edna had to speak up.

"This is impossible," she said and stood up in an instant. Her arms were waving, and she was so angry that these sisters could kidnap her and expect her to swallow such nonsense!

"Why would you make up such complete lies? For your own entertainment, I suppose!"

By then, Edna had turned and went straight for the door. Carol rushed to cut her off; the door was locked anyway.

"Edna, you should really sit back down and listen before you even think of leaving," Carol said.

Edna was fit to be tied.

"I want to go home and right now!" Edna said with blood rushing to her face and nearly fainting once again.

There was a pause of silence.

"Okay," Carol said. "We will take you home tomorrow if you promise to read a diary to prove what we say is true."

"Really, Edna said, how can I trust you to do that?"

Rosie took an old leather journal from its place in a locked desk drawer. As she handed it to Edna, she said softly, "Please read this book tonight, and if you still don't believe it, we shall take you back to your quiet, dismal life."

That night, after much deliberation, Edna picked up the leather-bound book. There were some odd symbols and some sort of poetry that could not be deciphered on the first page.

The second page was filled with scribbles and drawings of imaginary creatures. On the third page were the words.

And they shall look unto the earth and behold trouble, and darkness, dimness of anguish, and be driven to darkness.

Edna felt a chill come onto her. At once, she lost her haughty, dismissive mindset. Those words and the way the two women were tied to the crystal Oracle seemed like an omen. The word darkness was foreboding. Her instincts were sharpened. She wanted to read more but by only using caution.

Shadow's history was a legend that, if true, would shake up all former biological and scientific discoveries that were assumed to be fact.

The diary had been added to and passed on to women from generation to generation. The stories of Shadow's travels and influence on people she met were totally enthralling and, at the same time, frightening.

Shadow grew up knowing she was special. The most powerful men, royalty, generals, the excessively wealthy, and the largest meanest men she met would cower, not saying a word. They would avert their eyes after the shock of seeing her beautiful green eyes, perfect body, and regal presence.

Her voice had a perfectly controlled projection, almost but not quite too low for a lady.

Shadow didn't like men. The history of wars and violence brought about by men and not very smart men had turned her entire attitude to hatred. There was one person Shadow could not feel anything other than the strongest attraction to. This man was so perfect in every way that Shadow fell deeply in love.

She gave birth to a beautiful baby girl. She decided to raise the child herself and struck out for new adventures. This pattern of girls was repeated for 500 years; each one was blessed with the same powers as Shadow. The stories were all about the miracles and wonderful things each descendant passed on to the next female.

Edna stopped reading; it was late, and hours had passed. She walked up and walked over to the crystal window and was captivated by the full moonlight glistening on the calm waters of the sea. She fell asleep for a time and when she awoke found the book was in her lap. That's funny; she thought she was sure she had placed it on the footstool where she sat. Nearly finished with the successive additions to the stories, Edna was startled when she read about the twin girls.

Morning came, and she had slept well. Upon rising, she picked up the book and reread the ending pages; the last entry she read was:

This is Alice, I'm writing to pass on this information to the one reading it to herself.

I enjoyed my life and was happy and even fortunate to share the fantastic experience of having the bloodline of Shadow. I gave birth to twin girls; they had the same powers that were passed down through the many lifetimes after Shadow. However, I soon found that power and all it contained were only present when they were together.

For the first time, I felt to blame, having failed to produce just one girl. I felt twins would end the powers that had gone on for centuries. Their names were Eva and Vicki. Vicky was a lot more mischievous and scheming than Eva, who was the opposite and was very kind and considerate of others. Vicki could take control when they were together and cause upsets and unpredictable, dangerous situations. I decided to separate them as far apart as possible. I placed one in a very poor family. The other twin, I made sure, would grow up in a tiny village with little chance of leaving once she grew up.

I changed her name to Edna.

The next day, with Wilford's keen sense of direction guided by his instincts, they got closer; he had a feeling Elmer's mother was nearby. They were way off course from ocean shipping lanes, and since there were no other islands nearby, they stopped and hovered several miles away from Oracle Island.

Wilford said, "We will need a plan before we try to rescue Edna."

"Well, Elmer said, can we send Eyeball to scout around with a camera strapped to himself?"

"That's a capital idea," Wilford said.

And so, eyeball, their friendly bird did just that.

"Wow," said Bailey. "How can we ever hope to figure out where Edna is?"

The video that Eyeball brought back showed two castle-like towers separated by a bridge. Each tower had a crystal bubble on the top. Upon looking closer, Elmer noticed his mother inside one of the bubbles! And two women could be seen as well.

"Why would someone take Elmer's mother and bring her way out here?" Oskar asked.

"We won't know until we get her back," Wilford said.

Elmer said, "I think we will just have to ask those ladies why."

Wilford thought about that and could not see any way to pull off a daring rescue.

Carol noticed Eyeball flying around outside. Instantly, Rosie and herself knew what was going on. They could not allow Edna to leave just yet. The three of them left the bubble room and went down into the tower below. This fortress was formed from many metals and crystals that reached the ocean floor. It had many levels of living space. Both towers had voids where the lava had shrunk and separated, creating caves on the sides.

Edna was not yet told she was related to Shadow. She began to feel strange vibrations. Suddenly, it came to her: Rosie and Carol were related to her family in some way! Could it be she was also related to this Shadow person?

Once again, she felt woozy and nearly fainted.

Vicki had the exact same beauty Shadow had. If anything, she was even more perfect. The DNA kept its solid composition through the ages and expanded the cell's resilience, so her immune system repelled any nasty germs or virus mutations.

She also had no memory of her childhood or the teenage years, as did Edna.

The main difference between the two girls was that while Edna had no education other than a country high school, Vicky had struck out on her own and worked and finagled her way to graduate with honors from the most prestigious universities.

Power, especially over men and overly ambitious women, fed her desire to create an empire to be envied and feared.

"Why don't you take your international influence along with your reputation of being a hardnosed, super egotistical user of people's weakness and fall down an elevator shaft!"

Vicki had a way of letting bullies and insufferable wealthy people know to leave her alone. Friends were a waste of time, and she learned not to put any trust in so-called friends. Money never interested Vicki as much as the pleasure of being had squashing business magnates and those who tried to either join or beat her at her game of divide and conquer. That became more important than any other goal.

She had a master plan finally coming in line with her ambition to be a puppet master in a large and unforeseen monopoly.

Edna had reassured Elmer and his friend she was fine. She simply explained that she had a long-lost sister and was going to find her and then return home.

Edna moved to the city, and as much as she hated to leave Elmer on his own and her comfortable life, she needed to start the search for Vicki.

Without any office skills and only having a basic education, she was resigned to take a starting position as a shoe salesperson.

It was in a well-known department store, and after interviewing with the manager, Edna was hired on the spot.

The first day at work was disturbing. The other employees were not so friendly to her.

Her natural beauty and poise were usually mistaken for someone not genuine and only hired as window dressing. The competition for sales bonuses was very stiff, and Edna was a threat by being so attractive and with her calm, friendly personality to match.

Six months went by, and Edna had no clue how to locate her twin sister. The story of Shadow and the extended genealogy up to herself kept haunting her.

She had not been in contact with Rosie and Carol for all that time.

Edna was discouraged and ready to call them not with good news but with bad as a failure.

As she was taking a break in the stock room, she noticed all the shoeboxes were from the same company. So many styles of men, women, and children. She went back to work, not thinking much about it, not having had other jobs in the shoe business to compare.

The next day, she lost her job. There were complaints from jealous coworkers and some from friends of store employees. It seems stories and arguments were made up in a conspiracy to get Edna fired!

"Well, that's it," she said to herself. It looked like a dead end, and so she was planning to go back to her little cottage.

She thought maybe she should stay a little longer. Now, having shoe sales experience, there was no problem finding a job. It was in an even bigger store than the previous one.

In fact, it was a super shoe store known to be the largest and most respected shoe outlet on the East Coast.

She was excited to be the new person there and was warmly welcomed.

Once again, she was taking a break with another worker and suddenly noticed all the shoe boxes were from the same supplier. They did have different colors to identify the different styles and men from women.

After handling so many boxes every day, Edna never stopped to read the label and thought she recognized the logo. Two circles, with one on top in yellow and the bottom one a silhouette of a leafless tree. The same as the symbols she saw in the family history book! SHADOW SHOES. There was no other printing as to the company information, only the relevant size, style, and color.

Tracking SHADOW SHOES was nearly an impossible task. Not only was the company not listed directly, but the trail faded into the after a few dead ends. Also, Edna had no experience with the intricacies of computers and the Internet. She decided to start at the bottom, the delivery drivers.

They were almost never the same, and she had no time for her questions; after some mentions of a warehouse and following a company tuck with no name, Edna stopped at a locked gate. There was a large single-story building set back about fifty yards from the high-security fence. There was a guard house further down with thick thorny bushes lining the concrete wall. It reminded her of a prison.

Edna went home right after work and called Oracle Island.

"I think I've found Vicki!"

Rosie and Carol were more excited than Edna and wanted to know exactly where Vicki was. "Where is she?" They both asked at the same time.

"Well, I'm not sure, but I found a building that's connected to her in some way."

Rosie said, "If you take a picture of the building, we can use the Oracle and maybe find out more."

Later that day, as they were searching the Oracle, they were very surprised at what they found. The photo Edna had sent was also the same as many more located in all major cities on Earth.

"This is so strange," Carol said. "All these buildings. with security gates and no address signs!" Vicki's phone flashed. It was one of many special numbers she had to keep in contact with.

"It's Harold; I thought you should know someone has been taking photos and video of your plant at this location."

The monitor screen picked up the satellite image and then zoomed in to capture the person standing outside the gate at factory SB-1949-46. The letters and numbers indicated the location and facility number of over 1,000 such buildings.

Vicki jumped to her feet and calmly said to Harold. "I want you to notify our team there and have them bring that person to me at my main once."

Edna was greeted at the main entrance of a large multi-story building in New York City.

From there, it was an elevator ride to the top floor.

The lady accompanying her politely stepped out first. They then took another elevator, which had a code.

Edna asked as the lift stopped. "Who am I meeting?"

"I don't have that information." The lady answered as she stepped out and pointed to an open door.

Edna went into a spacious office with a commanding view of The Big Apple.

Edna sat down in the only empty chair facing a row of computer screens on the other side of the desk.

It looked like a smaller version of a TV production set.

Vicki sat with her back towards Edna. Not turning around, she said.

"Why were you taking video at the company's property the other day?"

Edna felt tiny and intimidated. She didn't know how to answer.

Vicky turned her chair and faced Edna.

"You aren't in trouble. I only want to know who told you to spy…" Vicky paused and looked Edna over.

"Who are you? Do I know you from somewhere?"

Edna knew she had finally found her twin sister.

In an instant, they saw each other's lives flash through their minds at the same time.

It was several minutes before either one could speak.

"We must have dinner tonight; I will pick you up at 7:00," Vicki said.

At dinner, Edna could not figure out what Vicki was doing with so many shoe factories. Once they got seated, Edna said to Vicki, "What's going on in the shoe business?"

Vicki Took a sip from her glass, set it down, and spoke.

"I'm not sure what sort of life you had growing up, but I'll tell you about mine."

Vicki leaned forward so only Edna could hear.

"I was left with a poor family of five other children in a third-world country of misery and squalor with little hope of surviving. I, like you, did not know I had a twin. The only thing I remember from my past during those times was that I did not have any shoes to wear. Consequently, I suffered infected feet so badly and, with no medical care, nearly lost my feet. I was in a coma for some time; they told me I had nearly died."

Edna was embarrassed; her memories were of happiness. Yes, she was also from a poor family, but they had plenty of what they needed.

She said to Vicki. "So, what is your plan, Sister?"

Vicki went into a business mode, and her voice changed.

"Worldwide market for shoe sales is now around $352 billion. That includes the five major continents, online sales in all categories such as ordinary footwear, athletic, fashion, and all other styles of shoes being sold."

Vicky enjoyed Edna's total undivided attention and was smug, knowing that Edna had no idea what her plan was.

She said, "I am going to let you in on my plan because you'll know it anyway."

"It's not the money. It's the power. Think about the basic article people in most of the world absolutely must have: Shoes! Imagine if your shoes wore out and you couldn't get any to replace them. The shoe industry relies on many materials such as rubber, plastic, fabric, nylon, metals, and who knows what else. Once my factories all over the world stop producing Shadow Shoes and supplies dry up, not only will people suffer as I did with no shoes to wear, but the whole supportive industry will also collapse."

Edna was silent.

She was trembling; her life in a small village with limited knowledge of the outside world caused her to nearly faint once again. The complex effects of Vicki's plan were almost too much for her to comprehend.

Edna sat back; she was incredulous. She asked Vicki.

"So, what do you hope to gain? I must say you have overcome and accomplished what should have been impossible."

"My master plan is finally coming together with my ambition to be a puppet master in a large and vital industry. I DESERVE TO TAKE CONTROL FROM FOOLS WHO HAVE MESSED UP THIS WORLD!"

After listening to Vicki's detailed description and getting more excited, Edna felt a black cloud coming over her. Her vision went sideways, and in a fit of vertigo, Edna fainted and fell to the floor.

When she woke up in an emergency room alone that evening, Edna forgot where she was. Vicki had called an ambulance and stayed in her office instead of following her to the hospital.

The entire conversation with her sister seemed so unreal. She believed it was a dream.

Vicki called and reminded her of what was said.

Carol and Rosie, we're preparing to travel to New York City. They wanted to meet Vicki and see just what kind of power the twins had together now that they had rejoined. They had no idea that the well-laid plans for taking their place in history as rulers were about to be smashed.

"I do hope you are going to be discharged soon; we have a lot of work to do," Vicki said.

Edna felt the same darkness overcome her and said, "Vicki, I can't understand why you need me. It seems you have everything in place."

"You don't understand. Carol and Rosie are coming here, and with our special power of seeing the future and with their crystal Oracle, we can totally bring peace to the world!"

"YOU CAN'T DO THAT! Your quest for power and glory is not what Shadow passed along. She would never disrupt the lives of millions by upsetting the world's supply of anything! What's next? The shipping lanes, the communication network? There is nothing that will make me be a part of this, and without me, your plan will fail!"

All along the way home, Edna was so relieved to be away from Vicki and especially Carol and Rosie. The thought of Vicki's bizarre plan to control the people and the resources all over the world made her shiver with icy chills.

The next day, Edna got back to her little country cottage after a long journey from New York.

It was late. She saw that a light was on inside.

That's odd, she thought because Elmer would be asleep at this hour.

Edna opened the door and, sitting in her knitting chair, was the same woman who had escorted her to Vicki's office. Before she could speak, the woman said.

"I believe we have your son, Elmer Van Pringle; you must come with me if you want to ever see him again."

"What," Edna said, "where?"

"ORACLE ISLAND."

THE END

Barnard